HELLO! WELCOME TO THE FABUMOUSE WORLD OF THE THEA SISTERS!

Thea Sisters

Hi, I'm Thea Stilton, Geronimo Stilton's sister! I am a special reporter for The Rodent's Gazette, the most famouse newspaper on Mouse Island. I love traveling and meeting new mice all over the world, like the Thea Sisters. These five friends have helped me out with my adventures. Let me introduce you to these fabumouse young mice!

Pamela loves pizza so much she eats it for breakfast. She is a skilled mechanic who can fix just about any motor she gets her paws on.
PAULINA is shy and loves to read about faraway places. But she loves traveling to those places even more.
Nicky is from the Australian Outback, where she developed a love of nature and the environment. This outdoors-loving mouse is always on the move.
Thea Sisters

Thea Stilton

MOUSEFORD ACADEMY

A DREAM ON ICE

Scholastic Inc.

www.geronimostilton.com

Published by Scholastic Inc., 557 Broadway, New York, NY 10012.

ISBN 978-0-545-91797-1

Text by Thea Stilton
Original title *Un sogno sul ghiaccio per Colette*
Cover by Giuseppe Facciotto
Illustrations by Barbara Pellizzari (pencils) and Francesco Castelli (color)
Graphics by Yuko Egusa

Special thanks to Tracey West
Translated by Lidia Morson Tramontozzi
Interior design by Becky James

10 9 8 7 6 5 4 3 2 1 16 17 18 19 20

Printed in the U.S.A. 40
First printing 2016

WINTER BLUES

Just as the winter semester began at Mouseford Academy, a cold wind blew across Whale Island. The Thea Sisters, five students who admired the ADVENTUROUS Thea Stilton, huddled inside the cozy Lizard Club lounge.

"There's nothing to do but read and play checkers," complained Pam.

"It's too bad Headmaster de Mousus TURNED DOWN our proposal for the Winter Games," said Paulina. "That would have been fun."

"He said the games might interfere with our studies," said thoughtful Violet.

"But we're studying all the time now," Colette said with a sigh.

Athletic Nicky JUMPED up. "Well, just because we can't have winter games doesn't mean that we have to sit around all day," she reminded them. "I'm going to the gym for a workout!"

Colette watched her go and sighed. "It's too bad it's not cold enough yet for a **deep freeze**," she said. "Then we'd be able to go ice skating."

"Oh, that's right, Coco," Paulina said, remembering. "Weren't you a **competitive skater** when you were a mouselet?"

Colette's cheeks turned pink. "That was a long time ago," she said.

Suddenly, Nicky burst back in, her eyes  SHINING with excitement.

"It's snowing!" she announced.

SNOWBALL FIGHT!

It seemed like every rodent in the school put on a winter coat, SCARF, and mittens and ran outside to play in the SNOW.

Nicky playfully hurled a snowball at another student, a tall rodent named Craig.

"Gotcha!" she cried, as it hit him in the shoulder.

Pam grinned. "Nice!" she congratulated Nicky.

Violet and Paulina quickly got to work making a SNOWMOUSE. They used STONES to make eyes, a nose, a mouth, and buttons.

"What do you think?" Paulina asked Colette.

There!

Ha! Ha! Ha!
Gotcha!

Colette put a paw on her chin. "Hmm," she said. "There's something missing."

"Really?" asked Violet.

Colette grinned. "She just needs a touch of pink!" she announced. Then she took off her SCARF and draped it around the neck of the snowmouse.

"PERFECT!"

The Thea Sisters stayed outside in the snow until it started to grow DARK. Colette shivered.

"We should go inside for some hot cocoa," she suggested.

"And cookies!" Pam added. "All this snowball-making has made me HUNGRY."

So the five friends went inside and gathered in Pam and Colette's room. They sipped steaming cups of hot chocolate and munched on tasty cheddar cookies.

Paulina gazed out the window at the **falling snow**.

"It's so pretty," she said. "It reminds me of the MOUNTAINS back home in Peru."

"Does that mean winter's your favorite season?" Nicky asked her friend.

"It might be," Paulina replied thoughtfully. "I do like the cold."

"I like some things about winter," said Colette. "But I hate what the cold does to my hair! It gets so dry."

"I like summer best," said Pam. "My CAR never wants to start when it gets really cold out."

"And I have to give up my DAILY RUN when the paths ice over," Nicky added.

Violet nodded. "The cold weather makes my VIOLIN go off-key," she said with a frown.

Nicky sighed. "I wish Headmaster de Mousus would let us put on the WINTER GAMES. That would give us something positive to do during these long, DARK, winter days."

"I agree," said Violet. "There are so many interesting WINTER SPORTS — curling, skiing, ice skating . . ."

Paulina looked down at her phone. "Speaking of ice skating, I have news!" she said. "The school has just announced that the ice pond has frozen over. We can go skating tomorrow!"

TO THE ICE!

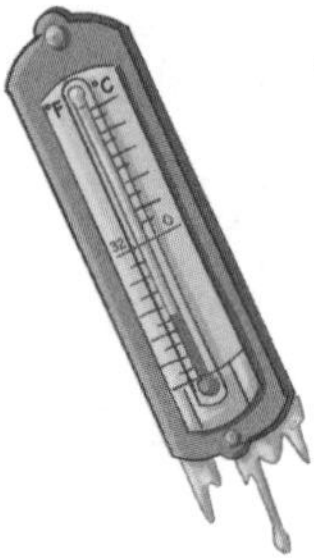

The next morning, all of Whale Island was covered with a glistening layer of frozen snow. Students spent the day longingly gazing out the window during classes. When classes ended, Headmaster de Mousus officially opened the ice-skating pond.

The Thea Sisters grabbed their skates and raced outside.

"I've never SKATED before, but I'll give it a TRY!" Pam exclaimed.

When they reached the pond, their friend Elly waved them over.

"Let's get a photo!" she called out,

holding up her camera, and the skaters **huddled** together for the shot.

"**Say cheese**!" Elly called, and then she took the picture.

A **cute** little mouselet was next to Elly: her little sister, Marina. She smiled when she saw Colette.

"Can you please help me skate today?" Marina asked.

"Of course!" Colette replied.

"Hey, where's Ruby?" Elly asked, as she lowered her camera. "She loves to skate!"

Ruby Flashyfur was one of the most **popular** students at the academy. Her family was also very rich.

"Here I am!" Ruby announced as she approached the group. "My mom had a SPECIAL skating jacket made just for me, and I was waiting for it to arrive. Isn't it fabumouse?"

She twirled around to show off the green jacket. Her name was spelled out in PINK RHINESTONES on the back.

Ruby **sailed** out onto the ice, **gliding** across the pond. Elly skated around, **snapping** pictures of everyone.

Pam's legs **wobbled** as she slowly skated onto the ice.

"Is this your first time, too?" asked shy Shen, who **wobbled** next to her.

"Get out of the way!" Craig yelled, **speeding** past them both. He and Nicky were playing **ICE HOCKEY**.

On the other side of the **frozen** pond, Colette led little Marina out onto the ice. Holding the mouselet's paws, she *patiently* helped her keep her balance.

When Marina was **steady**, Colette let go.

"Look! I'm really doing it!" Marina cried out **happily**. "I'm skating!"

AN UNEXPECTED GUEST

"**Go, Marina!**" Paulina cheered.

Violet skated up to her. "Colette is such a **GOOD TEACHER**."

"And a **good skater**," added Paulina. "I wonder why she stopped competing."

They were interrupted by a voice behind them.

"Excuse me," a female rodent said. "May I please **pass through**? I'd like to do some skating."

The two friends turned to see their literature teacher, Professor Rattcliff, standing there. She wore a cute **purple** skating outfit.

Professor Rattcliff wasn't the only

TEACHER who had gotten the idea to skate with the students. Professor Sparkle and Professor Marblemouse were **LACING UP** their skates as well.

But the biggest **SURPRISE** came when the school's dance teacher, Professor Plié, walked up to the pond. With her was a blond mouse who wore her hair in a ponytail.

Paulina's eyes grew wide. "That's Tara

Mousinski, the champion figure skater!"

Violet and Paulina HURRIED over to Professor Plié and the famouse skater.

"Professor!" exclaimed a very excited Paulina. "I didn't know you knew Ms. Mousinski."

"Call me Tara," the figure skater said with a smile. "Your professor is much more than a friend of mine. Without her help, I

never would have become a champion!"

Violet and Paulina exchanged **SURPRISED** glances.

"Really?" Violet asked. "We'd love to hear the whole story."

"Tara was one of my students," Professor Plié explained. "She had been **training** to become a professional figure skater ever since she was a tiny mouselet. She was

technically perfect, but often lost points for artistic performance."

Tara nodded. "As you know, Professor Plié is a wonderful dancer, and she really helped me improve the creative part of my routines," Tara said. "I've always been grateful to her for that. So whenever I get a chance, I come back to visit."

Then Tara's GAZE wandered to the ice. "Who is that skating with the little mouselet? She's very good."

Violet smiled proudly. "That's our friend Colette!"

A CIRCLE OF FRIENDS

Tara put on her skates and glided to meet Colette on the ice.

"You're a very graceful skater," Tara complimented her.

Colette BLUSHED. "Thank you. I took figure skating lessons for years."

"Colette used to skate in contests!" Marina piped up.

Tara's eyes LIT UP. "Really? Come on, do a spiral with me!"

"Well, I —" Colette started to protest, but Tara grabbed her paw. They skated across the pond together.

Nodding to each other, they LAUNCHED into the move. Each skater EXTENDED

her right leg behind her, knee bent, and grabbed her skate. Then both Tara and Colette glided forward on one skate!

The other skaters held paws and made a CIRCLE around the pair as they twirled on the ice. Ruby was the only one not to join the circle, **annoyed** because she was no longer the center of attention.

Ruby eyed Colette JEALOUSLY.

I know what I need to do, she thought. *I'll show Tara Mousinski that I'm the real skating star here at Mouseford!*

Humph!
Grab my paw!
I can do this!

You're doing great!
Whoa!

She **quickly** skated toward the circle, BREAKING THROUGH the skaters. Poor Pam lost her BALANCE and fell!

Ruby didn't care. She skated into the middle of the circle and began to spin.

Tara frowned and skated over to Ruby, a determined look on her snout.

"Excuse me, but that was very **rude**," she said. "No matter how **talented** a skater you are, you must **respect** every other skater on the ice!"

"I should have known you wouldn't **appreciate** my talent," Ruby shot back, skating off in a **HUFF**. "Fine! You can have the ice all to yourself. I'm tired of skating with **amateurs** anyway." Then she motioned to her group of friends, the **Ruby Crew** — Alicia, Zoe, and Connie. "Let's get out of here."

Nicky **helped** Pam back to her feet, and the skaters formed a circle again. Tara skated into the middle.

"So, who else wants to try a move with me?" she asked with a smile.

"I would!" Marina squeaked happily.

"You're on!" Tara replied as she offered her PAW to the tiny mouselet and led her to the middle of the ICE.

A MOUSETASTIC IDEA!

The Thea Sisters stayed at the pond for **HOURS**, skating with Craig and Shen.

"What a fabumouse day!" exclaimed Pam. "I'm so glad I finally learned how to skate."

"I don't think I quite got the hang of it," Shen admitted.

"We'll help you," Colette promised. Then she clapped her paws together. "I can't believe we skated with Tara Mousinski! She's so talented."

"And so **nice**, too," Paulina added.

"It would be great if we could do something special for her, to let her know how much we appreciate her visit," Violet said thoughtfully.

"I've got a **great** idea!" said Craig. "Let's get her some **cheese**!"

Paulina laughed. "That's nice, Craig, but maybe not quite **special** enough."

Nicky **frowned**. "It's too bad Headmaster de Mousus didn't **approve** our idea for the Winter Games. They'd be so much **FUN**,

and we could hold them in Tara's honor."

A voice piped up behind her.

"Did you say WINTER GAMES?" Professor Plié asked. She was standing there with Tara.

Nicky nodded. "We thought we could organize some **winter sports** competitions — you know, curling, ice hockey, figure skating . . ."

"But Headmaster de Mousus thought it would interfere with our studies," Paulina explained.

Professor Plié smiled. "Well, I think it's an excellent idea. Leave him to us."

The students followed Professor Plié and Tara to Headmaster de Mousus's office. The older mice went inside. They came out a few minutes later, followed by a beaming headmaster.

"Students, I have an announcement to make," he said. "Champion figure skater Tara Mousinski has just explained to me how participation in organized athletics can help students with academic performance. Therefore, I am pleased to announce that Mouseford Academy will hold its first WINTER GAMES!"

Whoa!
Hooray!
M

LET THE WORK BEGIN!

Soon, everyone on campus knew about the Winter Games. The next day, the Thea Sisters and other students gathered in the academy's newspaper office to start ORGANIZING the events. There was a lot to do!

"We should split up into groups," Nicky suggested. "We need a TEAM to make the POSTERS, and a team to come up with an event schedule . . ."

"First, we need to decide which events we will hold," Violet reminded her friend.

"I KNOW!" exclaimed Pam. "We can survey the students. I can create a poll online."

"Great idea!" agreed Nicky.

Pam quickly got to work, and by the

next afternoon, the results were in. Elly and her friend Tanja created a **colorful** event schedule.

"What do you think?" Elly asked, showing the *schedule* to Paulina. "Headmaster de Mousus said we could have a **long** weekend for the games. That's **FOUR DAYS**."

MOUSEFORD WINTER GAMES

DAY ONE	DAY TWO	DAY THREE	DAY FOUR
CROSS-COUNTRY SKIING	FIGURE SKATING (SHORT PROGRAM)	CURLING (SEMIFINALS)	CURLING (FINALS)
			FIGURE SKATING (LONG PROGRAM)

"CROSS-COUNTRY SKIING, **figure skating**, and **CURLING**," Paulina read out loud. "This is a great schedule! Thanks!"

Then Ruby and her friends walked in.

"**STOP** what you're doing, everyone!" Ruby announced.

Everyone stopped squeaking and turned toward Ruby.

"No schedules can be released without the **approval** of the Winter Games SPONSOR," Ruby replied.

"What do you mean *sponsor*?" PAULINA asked.

Ruby grinned. "I mean my **mother**,

CURLING

In curling, two teams of four players face each other on the ice. In each round, or end, one player pushes a granite stone toward a target. Other players sweep the ice in front of the stone to control its direction. The team with a stone closest to the bull's-eye earns points. The team with the most points after ten ends wins!

of course!" she said smugly. "She offered to sponsor the games, and Headmaster de Mousus was thrilled."

"Isn't it fabumouse?" chimed in Connie. "Mrs. Flashyfur is going to pay for all of the

posters and medals and everything else."

The Thea Sisters looked at one another. Now Ruby would be able to **BOSS** everyone around!

COLETTE'S SECRET

Of course, Mother!

Ruby's cell phone rang, and she quickly left the office.

"Oh, hello, Mother," she said. "No, don't worry. I'll WIN that figure skating competition."

"I'm COUNTING on you, Ruby," Mrs. Flashyfur told her daughter. "The events will be filled with reporters. When you win, it will ROCKET the Flashyfur name into the stratosphere and will help me SELL my new line of sportswear!"

"You can count on me, Mother," Ruby promised.

Excellent!

"Excellent, my **little cheeselet**," her mother said. "And be sure to smile your best for the photographers. Don't disappoint me!"

"I won't," Ruby said before she ended the call. She closed her eyes, imagining the GOLD MEDAL around her neck as photographers snapped her photo.

"There is no way the Thea Sisters can **BEAT ME** this time!" she muttered.

In the meantime, Colette had left the newspaper office and gone back to her room. She sat down at her dressing table and sighed.

Pam entered and saw Colette looking worried.

"What's up, Colette?" she asked.

"It's the GAMES," Colette replied. "I'm just not sure if I should enter the figure skating competition."

Pam raised her eyebrows. "Why not? You're the BEST skater at Mouseford! Besides, you used to COMPETE, right?"

"Thanks," Colette said, blushing. "But there's something I've never told **anyone** about my competition days."

"Ooh, a SECRET?" Pam asked.

Colette nodded. "During my last competition, everyone expected me to win FIRST PLACE," she explained. "I was sure I was going to win, too. But during my routine, I tripped and FELL."

"Oh no!" Pam cried.

"It happens to a lot of skaters," Colette said. "But I was really shaken up. I was so embarrassed! I finished my routine, but I had lost confidence and kept messing up. I came in LAST PLACE and never competed again."

"Poor Coco!" Pam said. "That must have been AWFUL! But that was a long time ago. You're older now, and you're a better skater."

"Do you really think so?" Colette asked.

"I know so!" her friend said confidently. "All you need is a little courage."

Just then Elly knocked on the door.

"Hey, Colette," she said, stepping inside the room. "Tara asked me to give you this."

She handed Colette a pink envelope. Colette opened it and read the note inside. She broke into a huge smile.

"What does it say?" Pam asked.

"I think I just found my courage!" Colette replied.

DEAR COLETTE,

I ENJOYED WATCHING YOU SKATE THE OTHER DAY. IT WAS ESPECIALLY NICE TO SEE YOU TEACH THAT YOUNG MOUSELET SO PATIENTLY. GOOD LUCK IN THE GAMES!

TARA

A GIFT OF MUSIC

Over the next two weeks, the students got ready for the games. Pamela and Paulina signed up for CROSS-COUNTRY SKIING. And Nicky formed a CURLING TEAM with Violet, Elly, and Shen.

Colette made up her mind to compete in figure skating, and she practiced every day after classes on the ice and in the gym. That's where Pam and Paulina found her one EVENING.

"Hey, Colette!" Pam called out as her friend practiced her moves.

Colette spun around. "Oh, hi! I didn't hear you come in."

"We brought you something," Pam said,

showing Colette her phone.

"Pam told me that you hadn't chosen your MUSIC yet," Paulina added. "So we made some selections for you and created a playlist."

Colette's eyes widened with SURPRISE.

"Thank you so much!" she squealed.

"Paulina chose some slow pieces," Pam explained. "And I picked some songs that were faster and more rhythmic."

Colette hugged her friends. "I'll listen to them tonight. I'm sure I'll find the perfect song for my routine."

"How's that courage coming?" Paulina asked. Colette had opened up to all the Thea Sisters about her competition nerves, and they'd all been very supportive.

"I'm feeling pretty good," Colette replied. "I'm just practicing all I can. I don't want to make any mistakes this time!"

"That's GREAT, Colette," Pam said encouragingly. "We can't wait to see you compete."

Colette felt lucky to have such fabumouse friends.

"How's your cross-country skiing practice been?" she asked them.

"Terrific!" Pam replied. "There's nothing better than gliding through the woods over fresh snow."

Then Nicky and Violet walked into the gym, frowning.

"You two look **SADDER** than rats in an empty cheese factory," Pam said. "What's wrong?"

MEET THE CRYSTALS

"We're okay," said Violet, but with a sad sigh that told her friends she wasn't being honest.

"Oh, come on, we can tell something's **bothering** you," Pam said.

"Ah, we've just had our confidence shaken, that's all," Nicky replied.

"We were practicing with our curling team, and then we saw ***THE INVINCIBLES*** train."

"The Invincibles?" Paulina asked.

"That's the name of Craig, Ryder, Ron, and Tanja's **CURLING TEAM**," Violet explained.

"And they chose the **RIGHT NAME**,"

added Nicky. "It doesn't look like they can be beaten!"

"Well, I was just telling Pam and Paulina that I'm building my **CONFIDENCE** with lots of practice," offered Colette. "Just keep at it!"

"And maybe you need a special name for your team, too," suggested Paulina.

"Yes, that's a **great idea**!" agreed Violet.

"Something to do with **ice**, maybe," said Pam, thinking.

The friends were quiet for a minute.

Paulina GAZED up at the pretty blue snowflake decorations hanging from the ceiling of the gym.

"I've got it!" she blurted out. "How about the Crystals?"

"That's just perfect!" squealed Nicky and Violet.

"And you need uniforms, right?" asked Colette, taking down one of the decorations. "Well, imagine a light blue shirt with a beautiful white snow crystal embroidered on it!"

How about this?

"That would be so nice," said Violet. "And I think Shen and Elly will like the idea, too."

We're a great team!

"I'm sure they will," agreed Nicky.

"You're such good friends," Violet said. "We've got a wonderful name and a uniform plan. I'm feeling more CONFIDENT already!"

Pam grinned. "Hey, the Thea Sisters make a great team — you know that!"

Paulina turned to Colette. "Do you have a costume for your skating routines yet?"

Colette shook her head. "Not yet. I've been too busy working on my routine. But I'll get around to it."

"I'm sure whatever you come up with will be fabumouse!" Pam said.

"I HOPE so," Colette replied. "And now, if you'll excuse me, I've got to get back to practice!"

AN EARLY-MORNING SURPRISE

The week before the games flew by in a **BLUR**! The students still had their normal classes, quizzes, and tests. In their free time, they worked hard organizing the games and **practicing** for events.

One morning, Colette woke up before the sun. She wanted to get in an early practice by herself, without having to RUSH. As she reached the **FROZEN** pond, the sun was just beginning to warm up the **snow-covered** landscape.

Colette soon saw that she was not **alone**.

Tara Mousinski was on the pond, skating effortlessly on the ice. Colette moved silently along the path, careful not to make any noise.

The swishing of Tara's blades on the ice seemed to create a beautiful melody that accompanied Tara in her dance. Colette watched, transfixed, as the skater launched into a perfect jump.

Colette couldn't help herself. She exploded in loud applause.

"Hey!" squeaked Tara when she realized that she wasn't alone.

Colette's paw flew to her mouth. "Sorry!"

Tara skated up to her. "No problem. Are you here to practice your routine?"

Colette nodded.

"Well, LET'S SEE IT!" Tara said.

Feeling a little nervous, Colette put on her skates and glided out onto the ice. Tara watched her carefully.

"Very nice," Tara said. "But you're a little short on jumps. You could add a few more."

"I know," Colette said. "It's just —"

Colette hadn't known Tara for long, but already she felt like a friend. So she told Tara the story of how she had wiped out during competition when she was younger.

"So I've been afraid to put advanced

jumps into my long program," Colette admitted.

"Well, you shouldn't be," said Tara. "You'll need to perform some advanced jumps if you want to win. Can you do a double axel?"

"I've tried it many times," Colette replied. "But it's so difficult! I've never landed without falling. I don't think I can do it."

"Let me show you," Tara said.

After circling the pond once she launched into the double axel, landing the jump perfectly.

DOUBLE AXEL

This is one of the most difficult moves in figure skating. The skater begins the jump facing forward, rotates two and a half times in the air, and then lands facing backward.

"That was amazing!" Colette exclaimed.

"It wasn't always this easy for me, you know," Tara explained. "The night before the national championship, I wiped out doing a double axel at practice. I couldn't sleep that night. And when it came time for the competition, I was almost too scared to make the jump."

"And what happened?" Colette asked.

Tara smiled. "I made the jump, and I won! And I know you can get your courage back, too."

Tara's story gave Colette the confidence she needed. "You're right!" she cried.

THE BIG DAY

The cold winter sun shone brightly on the morning the games began. Students, spectators, and reporters gathered early for the opening of the MOUSEFORD WINTER GAMES. The logo for Flashyfur Enterprises was visible everywhere.

The cross-country ski events were slated to START OFF the games. A crowd gathered in the clearing where the female skiers would begin their trek.

BOOMER WHALE, the Mouseford Academy handymouse, addressed the crowd through a MEGAPHONE.

"Attention, rodents!" he yelled. "Please clear the starting line and move behind the

START
Hooray!
Woo-hoo!
FF

barriers. The games are about to begin!"

"Boomer, I don't think you need the megaphone," Headmaster de Mousus said. "You're LOUD ENOUGH already!"

"What did you say?" Boomer SHOUTED into the megaphone, which was directly next to the headmaster's ear.

The dazed headmaster walked away to prepare his opening speech for the games.

Over on the sidelines, Colette, Violet, and Nicky gathered around Pam and Paulina, who were stretching to warm up before the race.

"Do you two have your lip balm?" Nicky asked.

"**Got it!**" Paulina and Pam replied.

"**Ski goggles?**" asked Violet.

"Got them!"

"**SUNSCREEN?**" asked Colette.

Pam and Paulina looked at each other. They had **forgotten** it!

"Don't worry, I've got some," Colette said, taking a tube from her bag. "You'll be out in the **winter sun** for a long time."

Then she covered her friends' snouts with the **lotion**.

Nearby, Ruby's friends were on the sidelines, waiting for the race to start. Zoe was sipping from a cup of **hot chocolate**.

"What's the **big deal** about crossing the island on a pair of skis?" she snorted. "It's such a waste of effort. I'll watch the start and then head back to my cozy room."

"Ah, there you are!" cried Ruby, running toward her. "Here's your JERSEY NUMBER. I signed you up for this event."

"What?" squeaked a startled Zoe. "Why?"

"What do you mean *why*?" Ruby asked. "We can't let the Thea Sisters WIN every event. My mother is counting on the Ruby Crew to win gold. I will destroy Colette in the figure skating competition, but you have to beat Pam and Paulina at cross-country skiing."

Are you kidding?

Zoe's EYES narrowed. "So does that mean you're going to sign up Connie and Alicia for CURLING?

They'll need to find two other players to form a team."

Ruby burst out laughing. "Curling's not a fashionable sport," she said. "I bet the **reporters** won't even cover it. We'll leave that one for the Thea Sisters."

"So then why am I the **only one** who has to ski?" Zoe complained.

"Don't worry, you'll be great!" Ruby said, PUSHING her friend forward. "Now go win that race!"

ON YOUR MARK, GET SET . . . GO!

Headmaster de Mousus was giving a speech and, as usual, it wasn't a short one.

"And it is my **HOPE** that these games will **UNIFY** the students of Mouseford Academy . . ."

CLAP! CLAP! CLAP!

The crowd burst into applause, thinking that the speech was finally over.

"Thank you, but I have **MUCH MORE** to say," the headmaster continued. "Now, another aspect of the games . . ."

"How long is this going to go on?" Paulina whispered to Pam.

"If he keeps going like this, the Winter Games will turn into the SUMMER GAMES!" Pam joked.

Finally, Headmaster de Mousus finished his long-winded speech.

"And so, without further ado, I'm delighted to open the Mouseford Winter Games with the female CROSS-COUNTRY SKIING competition!"

Boomer held the MEGAPHONE to his mouth and bellowed, "On your mark, get set . . . go!"

Spurred by the encouraging shouts of the crowd, the athletes TOOK OFF with a BURST of energy.

"Go, Paulina! Go, Pam!" CHEERED Nicky, Colette, and Violet.

"Go, Zoe!" Ruby shrieked. "Remember, you have to WIN!"

The race went along a trail that wound through the woods and CRISSCROSSED Whale Island.

Zoe took off like a CAT chasing her tail. She didn't realize that this race wasn't a *SPRINT*—it went for ten kilometers, or more than six miles! She also didn't realize that it might have been smarter to dole out her ENERGY over the whole race so she'd have something left to get to the finish line.

Zoe LOOKED behind her and saw that she had a huge lead.

"Good," she said wearily. "I'll just rest here for a minute."

Zoe removed her skis, left the trail, and sat down on the TRUNK of a fallen tree.

Behind her, Pam and Paulina were moving at a STEADY pace. They were enjoying the race and the GLORIOUS day. After a short while, they managed to take the LEAD together.

Zoe, who was sitting in a secluded spot, didn't see the other racers pass her.

RING! RING! RING!

"Hi, Ruby," she said, answering her cell phone. "Where am I? I'm, um, **in the lead**, of course!"

After lying to Ruby, Zoe put her skis back on and scurried to rejoin the racers.

When she got back on the path, she saw the **TRACKS** of the other skiers in the snow.

"I'm in **last place**," she realized. "Ruby will be so **cheesed off** at me! I'd better take a **shortcut** to catch up."

Then she skied off into the woods.

THREE CHEERS FOR THE WINNERS!

Nicky, Colette, and Violet waited at the **FINISH LINE**, practically jumping out of their fur with excitement. They knew the **FIRST** racers would be arriving soon.

Shen suddenly saw something. "**HEY!**" he shouted, pointing to a lone figure in the distance. "Isn't that Pam? She's in the lead!"

"Yes!" Colette cried, clapping her paws. "It's Pam!"

"**Impossible!**" snapped Ruby. "Take another look. That's got to be Zoe!"

But as the skier got closer, it was clearly PAMELA!

Everyone **cheered** as Pam *WHIZZED* across the finish line first, followed shortly

FINISH

after by Paulina. Reporters IMMEDIATELY surrounded the two winners.

Ruby watched the other skiers finish, one by one, yet there was still no sign of Zoe. She was FURIOUS!

"Where is that lazybones?" she asked Connie and Alicia. Then she dialed Zoe's number again, but this time, Zoe didn't answer.

Alicia and Connie exchanged worried glances. Where was Zoe?

In the meantime, the male contestants were LINED UP at the start of the race, ready to take off. Headmaster de Mousus announced the START of the race, with help from Boomer and his megaphone, and the racers TOOK OFF with Craig in the lead.

At the finish line, Paulina was finishing up an interview when she felt a paw tap her shoulder. She turned to see Alicia and Connie standing there.

"We need the Thea Sisters to help us," Alicia said.

"ZOE IS MISSING!"

RESCUE TEAM IN ACTION!

Ruby marched up. "Why are you bringing the Thea Sisters into this?"

Alicia shrugged SHEEPISHLY. "Well, they know how to get things done."

"This could be SERIOUS," Paulina said. "What if Zoe is hurt?"

"Then the male racers will see her," Ruby snapped. "Let's just WAIT for them to get back."

Paulina and Pam went to find Nicky, Violet, and Colette. Together, they WAITED for the second round of racers to return.

Craig was the first racer to cross the finish line. As the reporters crowded around him, Paulina PUSHED her way through.

"Congratulations!" she told him. "I was just wondering if you saw Zoe on the trail. She never FINISHED her race."

Craig shook his head. "No. There was nobody on the path."

Paulina cast an anxious glance at the sun, which was low in the sky. Then she headed back to the Thea Sisters.

"Craig didn't see Zoe," she reported. "And it's getting dark."

"We should go LOOK for her right away," Nicky said. "But first we'll need some supplies."

They quickly sprang into action. First, Violet informed Headmaster de Mousus that they were forming a SEARCH PARTY for Zoe.

Nicky rounded up some flashlights, Colette found a blanket, and Pam filled a

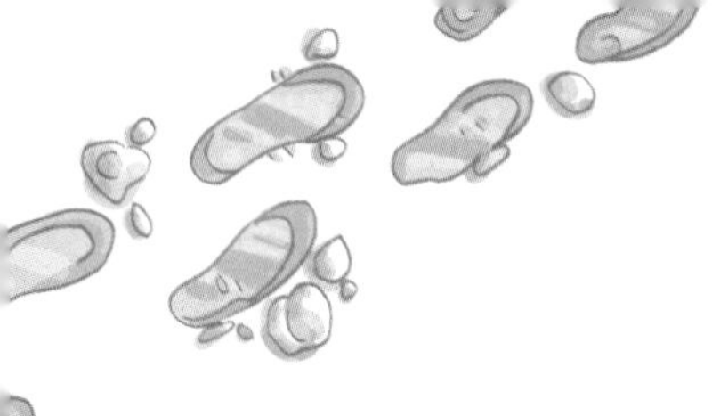

thermos with **hot chocolate**.

"Let's go find Zoe!" Paulina said.

Alicia and Connie slipped away from Ruby and gave Paulina a **hug**.

"Thank you," Alicia said. "I **HOPE** you find her!"

The Thea Sisters headed out on the trail.

"What could have happened to her?" Violet wondered.

"She might have **LEFT THE TRAIL** and couldn't find her way back," Nicky guessed. "With all this snow, even familiar places look *strange*!"

"I have a **MAP** of the race trail, so we won't get lost," Paulina promised.

They walked and walked, until Pam squeaked. "**LOOK!** Is that Zoe's hat?"

"It is!" Colette agreed. "Hopefully she's nearby."

They began calling out Zoe's name. A feeble voice answered in the distance.

"Help! I'm here!"

They RACED to her. Nicky wrapped Zoe in a blanket, and Violet handed her the hot chocolate.

"Thanks," said Zoe. "I tried to take a shortcut and I got lost. I never should have entered the race!"

YOU CAN DO IT, COLETTE!

That night, Colette tossed and turned in her sleep. The next day, she would skate her short program. The performance had to contain required

MOVES and **jumps**, and she would be scored by how well she executed them.

She woke up early, put on her skating costume, and headed for the frozen pond. Seated at the judges' table were Professor Aria, Professor Plotfur, Professor Ratyshnikov, Professor Plié, and Tara Mousinski.

Colette took a deep breath and **warmed up** on the ice. The most **difficult** required jump in this short program was a move called a double lutz.

"You can do it, Colette!" her friends CHEERED from the stands.

Colette smiled. She could do this!

Her music started, and she began her routine.

The hours of practice had paid off. Colette performed her routine **CONFIDENTLY**. When it came time for the double lutz, she *gracefully* spun twice in the air and landed *smoothly* on one skate. She'd done it!

The judges gave her a good **SCORE**, which would be added to her score for the long program in two days. The crowd **CHEERED** as she skated off the ice, smiling.

The following morning, Colette woke up *early* to practice her long program. As she twirled around the pond, she heard a voice.

Yay, Colette!

"COLETTE IS THE BEST!" cheered Elly's little sister.

"Marina! Thank you,"

Colette said, skating toward her. "But what are you doing here by yourself?"

The mouselet grinned. "We have a SURPRISE for you," she said.

"We?" Colette asked, and then she saw the other THEA SISTERS walking down the path: Nicky and Violet were wearing light blue pullovers with crystal snowflakes on the front.

"Wow!" Colette cried. "The Crystals uniform came out great! You look amazing."

"Thank you," said Violet. "We're heading over to the semifinal rounds soon for our first match."

"And the uniforms were your idea," added Nicky. "So we came up with a little gift for you."

Pam took out a bag she had been hiding behind her back. She removed a delicate

outfit. Colette gasped. Her friends had given her a stunning ice-skating costume! It had a pretty pink bodice and a flouncy light blue skirt.

"I . . . I don't know what to say," Colette stammered. "This is beautiful! And I've been so busy practicing that I was just going to wear the same outfit twice. This is perfect. Thank you!"

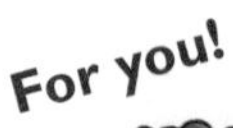

Then Marina shyly handed a package to Colette. Inside was a hair comb that matched the costume.

"It's beautiful!" Colette exclaimed.

"I made it myself," said Marina.

Colette hugged the little mouselet. Then she looked at the Thea Sisters.

"You really are the **best friends** in the world," she said. "Thank you for CHEERING me on yesterday."

"You did great!" said Nicky. "And you **didn't fall** once!"

Colette nodded. "I know. But Tara thinks I should try a more difficult move in my long program, a DOUBLE AXEL. Every time I practice it, I fall."

"Keep practicing," Pam urged her. "We **know** you can do it!"

"And we'll support you all the way," Violet chimed in.

"Go, Colette," Marina cheered sweetly.

DISAPPOINTMENTS AND VICTORIES

"If you don't mind, I'm going to stay here and keep working," Colette said. "**Good luck** with your match!"

"No worries," Nicky said, and the mice headed off to the **CURLING MATCH**.

Alone on the pond, Colette practiced the double axel **again** and **again**. She **jumped** and she **jumped** . . . and each time, she fell! She got up **again** and **again**, until finally, she gave up.

"**It's no use!**" she cried. "I'll never be able to do it."

Then she heard the

sound of happy squeaking coming toward her.

"Hooray for the Crystals! Hip, hip . . .

HOORAY!"

Pam, Paulina, Violet, Nicky, Elly, Marina, and Shen came toward the pond, CHEERING and bursting with ENERGY.

They won!

"**YOU WON!**" Colette cried.

"Yes, they sure did!" exclaimed Pam.

"We got into the finals, and we're going to face off against ***THE INVINCIBLES*** tomorrow," Nicky said. "That should be interesting."

"Oh, and the reporters **loved** our

uniforms," added Violet. "They took lots of pictures. That seemed to bother Ruby for some reason."

"How about you, Coco?" Paulina asked. "How did practice go?"

Colette didn't want to SPOIL their excitement, so she tried to hide her disappointment about not being able to master the double axel.

"Great!" she said, smiling. "But I think I'll take the DOUBLE AXEL out of my choreography. I don't think I'll be able to do it."

Violet put a paw on her shoulder. "With or without it, I'm sure you'll give a wonderful performance," she said.

I hope so, Colette thought.

An Unforgettable Victory

"It's the final day of the MOUSEFORD WINTER GAMES!" Boomer announced over the megaphone the next morning.

The excitement at the academy was electric. Everyone was eager to see who would win the GOLD MEDALS in curling and figure skating.

The Crystals headed for the curling arena early to practice, and Colette went back to the pond. She was going over her routine when Ruby skated onto the ice. She was wearing a green-and-blue skating costume with gold cap sleeves.

Ruby stopped in her tracks when she saw Colette practicing her program. She had

already seen Colette do well in the short program, and her skating this time looked even better! Defeating Colette was not going to be as easy as she thought.

"Hi, Ruby!" Colette called out, skating over to her. "I'm done. The pond is all yours if you want to practice."

Humph!

Ruby folded her arms with a huff. "Why would I practice with nobody watching?" she asked. "My PUBLIC will be arriving at any moment."

Colette raised an eyebrow. "Your public?"

"My mother let the press know that I would be coming here to practice," Ruby replied. "I should be swarmed by reporters any minute."

"Actually, all the **press** is at the curling arena," Colette told her. "It's the **MAIN EVENT** this morning. That's where I'm headed right now! See you later."

Colette took off her skates and headed to the curling match. Ruby frowned. How could a SILLY sport like curling take away her press? It wasn't **fair**!

"Achoo!" Ruby sneezed. She had worn

her costume for the reporters, and now she was catching a cold!

Leaving Ruby behind, Colette **hurried** to the outdoor arena where the curling course had been set up on the ice. As she climbed the bleachers, she saw the Crystals getting ready to face *THE INVINCIBLES*. Craig, Ryder, Ron, and Tanja had gotten creative with their uniforms, too. They all wore short SUPERHERO CAPES!

The crowd QUIETED DOWN as the match began. It was a close game. The Crystals won the first end, and *THE INVINCIBLES* won the second end. The match went BACK AND *FORTH* like this until the finish of the ninth end. Each

team had **FOURTEEN POINTS**!

You could hear a **cheese crumb** drop. When Violet gave the final stone a *PUSH*, Elly and Nicky **swept** the ice as the stone slid toward the target. It landed right in the **CENTER**!

RUBY'S PLAN

That night, spotlights shone on the ice pond, and it SPARKLED like a new mirror. Spectators and reporters squeezed into the packed bleachers. Everyone was curious to see who would win the Mouseford GOLD MEDAL in the figure skating competition.

Rebecca Flashyfur was there, keeping her EYES on her daughter. So far, the reporters had been writing mainly about the THEA SISTERS! But she was counting on Ruby to WIN.

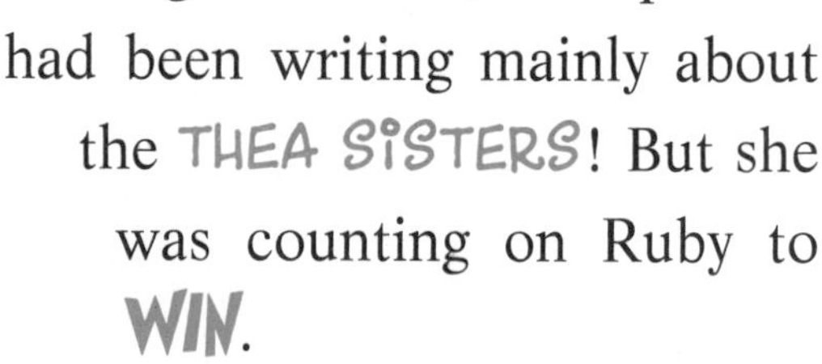

Ruby and Colette sat on a bench near the pond, getting ready to skate.

"I hope my **choreography** will be enough," Colette muttered to herself. She still felt **uneasy** about her decision to drop the double axel.

Ruby saw her mother in the stands and started to feel **nervous**. She had to win. She couldn't chance it. Unless . . .

"Excuse me, Colette, may I **borrow** your

hairbrush, please? I left mine in my room," Ruby asked sweetly.

"Sure," Colette replied, and began to dig in her duffel bag to find it. While Colette wasn't LOOKING, Ruby quickly SLICED through one of the shoelaces on Colette's skate — not all the way, but enough so that it would BREAK during Colette's performance.

"Now everything will be okay," Ruby said under her breath.

"What did you say?" Colette asked, looking up from her bag.

"Oh, nothing!" Ruby replied quickly. "I was just saying that you really look okay!"

TROUBLE ON THE ICE!

Ruby's fans cheered her on as she skated onto the ice, the first to perform.

"GO, RUBY!" Connie yelled. "You're the best!"

Go, Ruby!

An AGGRESSIVE beat blasted from the speakers as Ruby's performance music filled the air. Ruby began her program, a FAST-PACED routine with PRECISE movements and dizzying twirls.

"That's my little mouselet!" Mrs. Flashyfur PROUDLY called out.

"**Great moves!**" remarked Tara at the judges' table.

"She's like a VOLCANO," echoed Professor Plié. "That was a truly powerful performance!"

The rest of the judges agreed, and they all gave Ruby high scores. Colette quickly did the math in her head. She would need a near-perfect performance if she wanted to beat Ruby!

"I'll have to do the DOUBLE AXEL after all," she realized — and she realized something else, too. She wasn't nervous! She looked up at her CHEERING friends in the stands and smiled.

You have practiced. Your friends are rooting for you. You can do this! she told herself.

A slow, classical piece came over the speakers. At the first note, Colette skated lightly and gracefully across the ice.

Colette LAUNCHED into her first jump — and crashed face-first onto the ice when she landed!

At that moment, her past came flooding back. She remembered FALLING when she was younger. Dazed, Colette sat up and noticed her broken shoelace on the ice. She waved to the judges.

"I need to STOP!" Colette cried out.

A SECOND CHANCE

Colette got up and LIMPED back to the bench. Her friends were waiting for her.

"Are you okay?" Violet asked, her eyes wide with worry.

"My shoelace broke," Colette replied. "If I can't repair it within two minutes, I'll be disqualified."

Paulina took the skate and the shoelace from Colette. "Hmm," she said. "I'll be right back."

Paulina brought the skate to the judges. A few minutes later, she returned with Tara.

"Colette, the judges have determined that your lace was sliced on purpose," she said. "You've been sabotaged!"

Colette gasped. "Really? But who would do such a thing?"

Pam glanced over at Ruby. "Oh, I've got an idea," she said.

"It's likely, but we can't prove it," Paulina said. "The **good news** is, Colette, that you won't lose **points** for the fall. You can **begin** your program again."

Colette sighed. "I would if I could," she said. "But it looks like my blade was damaged when I fell. And I don't have another pair of skates."

Tara smiled. "Of course you do," she said. "You can borrow mine!"

DON'T EVER GIVE UP!

"Colette will begin her program from the start!" Headmaster de Mousus **ANNOUNCED**. "She will not be **penalized** for the fall."

A murmur went through the crowd. Ruby shifted UNCOMFORTABLY in her seat.

"She had better not outscore you," Mrs. Flashyfur snapped at her daughter.

Colette laced up Tara's skates. Her mind **FLASHED BACK** to those years ago. She had been so **shaken** after that fall!

You were different then, Colette told herself. *You were only a mouselet. And you didn't have the Thea Sisters to support you!*

"**GO, COLETTE! YOU'RE THE BEST!**" shouted Marina from the stands.

Colette smiled up at her and glided back out onto the ice. She stopped in the center of the pond, under a beam of GOLDEN LIGHT. She gazed up at her friends. Seeing the ENCOURAGEMENT in their faces gave her confidence.

The music started and Colette began her program. She did her first jump and made a perfect landing! Then Colette skated across the ice. It was time for her double axel.

The crowd was silent as Colette rocketed

into the air, spinning two and a half times and landing flawlessly. Then they burst into **THUNDEROUS** applause.

Colette's heart **pounded** as she finished her program to more applause. The judges gave their **FINAL SCORES**, and Headmaster de Mousus declared the winner.

"Colette and Ruby are *tied* for the gold!"

Reporters **swarmed** the two skaters.

"*Colette! Colette!*" one shouted. "Give us a quote!"

"I dedicate this performance to my friends, the THEA SISTERS!" she said tearfully. "I couldn't have done this without them!"

This is for the Thea Sisters!

Don't miss any of these exciting Thea Sisters adventures!

Thea Stilton and the Dragon's Code

Thea Stilton and the Mountain of Fire

Thea Stilton and the Ghost of the Shipwreck

Thea Stilton and the Secret City

Thea Stilton and the Mystery in Paris

Thea Stilton and the Cherry Blossom Adventure

Thea Stilton and the Star Castaways

Thea Stilton: Big Trouble in the Big Apple

Thea Stilton and the Ice Treasure

Thea Stilton and the Secret of the Old Castle

Thea Stilton and the Blue Scarab Hunt

Thea Stilton and the Prince's Emerald

Thea Stilton and the Mystery on the Orient Express

Thea Stilton and the Dancing Shadows

Thea Stilton and the Legend of the Fire Flowers

Thea Stilton and the Spanish Dance Mission

Thea Stilton and the Journey to the Lion's Den

Thea Stilton and the Great Tulip Heist

Thea Stilton and the Chocolate Sabotage

Thea Stilton and the Missing Myth

Thea Stilton and the Lost Letters

Thea Stilton and the Tropical Treasure

Thea Stilton and the Hollywood Hoax

Don't miss any of my fabumouse special editions!

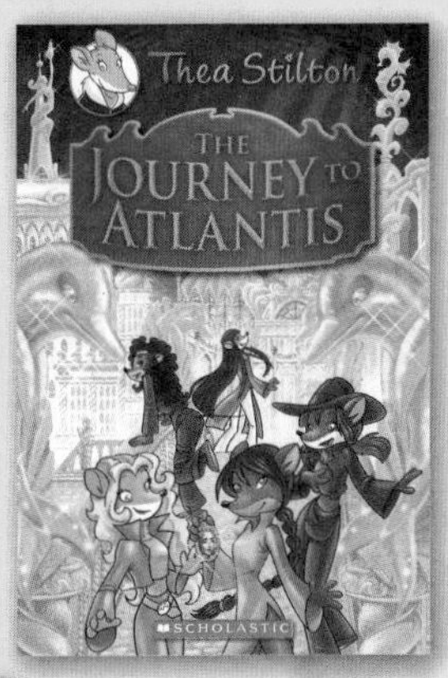

THE JOURNEY TO ATLANTIS

THE SECRET OF THE FAIRIES

THE SECRET OF THE SNOW

THE CLOUD CASTLE

Be sure to read all my fabumouse adventures!

#1 Lost Treasure of the Emerald Eye

#2 The Curse of the Cheese Pyramid

#3 Cat and Mouse in a Haunted House

#4 I'm Too Fond of My Fur!

#5 Four Mice Deep in the Jungle

#6 Paws Off, Cheddarface!

#7 Red Pizzas for a Blue Count

#8 Attack of the Bandit Cats

#9 A Fabumouse Vacation for Geronimo

#10 All Because of a Cup of Coffee

#11 It's Halloween, You 'Fraidy Mouse!

#12 Merry Christmas, Geronimo!

#13 The Phantom of the Subway

#14 The Temple of the Ruby of Fire

#15 The Mona Mousa Code

#16 A Cheese-Colored Camper

#17 Watch Your Whiskers, Stilton!

#18 Shipwreck on the Pirate Islands

#19 My Name Is Stilton, Geronimo Stilton

#20 Surf's Up, Geronimo!

#21 The Wild, Wild West

#22 The Secret of Cacklefur Castle

A Christmas Tale

#23 Valentine's Day Disaster

#24 Field Trip to Niagara Falls

#25 The Search for Sunken Treasure

#26 The Mummy with No Name

#27 The Christmas Toy Factory

#28 Wedding Crasher

#29 Down and Out Down Under

#30 The Mouse Island Marathon

#31 The Mysterious Cheese Thief

Christmas Catastrophe

#32 Valley of the Giant Skeletons

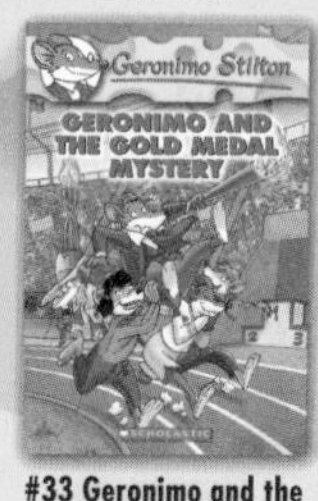

#33 Geronimo and the Gold Medal Mystery

#34 Geronimo Stilton, Secret Agent

#35 A Very Merry Christmas

#36 Geronimo's Valentine

#37 The Race Across America

#38 A Fabumouse School Adventure

#39 Singing Sensation

#40 The Karate Mouse

#41 Mighty Mount Kilimanjaro

#42 The Peculiar Pumpkin Thief

#43 I'm Not a Supermouse!

#44 The Giant Diamond Robbery

#45 Save the White Whale!

#46 The Haunted Castle

#47 Run for the Hills, Geronimo!

#48 The Mystery in Venice

#49 The Way of the Samurai

#50 This Hotel Is Haunted!

#51 The Enormouse Pearl Heist

#52 Mouse in Space!

#53 Rumble in the Jungle

#54 Get into Gear, Stilton!

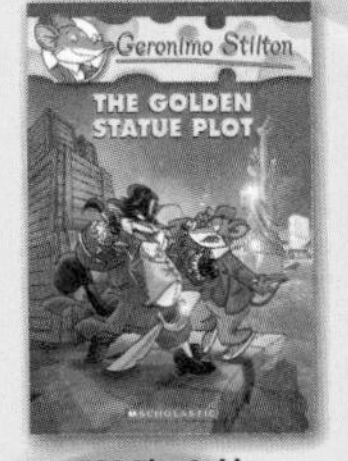

#55 The Golden Statue Plot

#56 Flight of the Red Bandit

The Hunt for the Golden Book

#57 The Stinky Cheese Vacation

#58 The Super Chef Contest

#59 Welcome to Moldy Manor

The Hunt for the Curious Cheese

#60 The Treasure of Easter Island

#61 Mouse House Hunter

#62 Mouse Overboard!

The Hunt for the Secret Papyrus

#63 The Cheese Experiment

Don't miss any of these Mouseford Academy adventures!

#1 Drama at Mouseford

#2 The Missing Diary

#3 Mouselets in Danger

#4 Dance Challenge

#5 The Secret Invention

#6 A Mouseford Musical

#7 Mice Take the Stage

#8 A Fashionable Mystery

#9 The Mysterious Love Letter

#10 A Dream on Ice

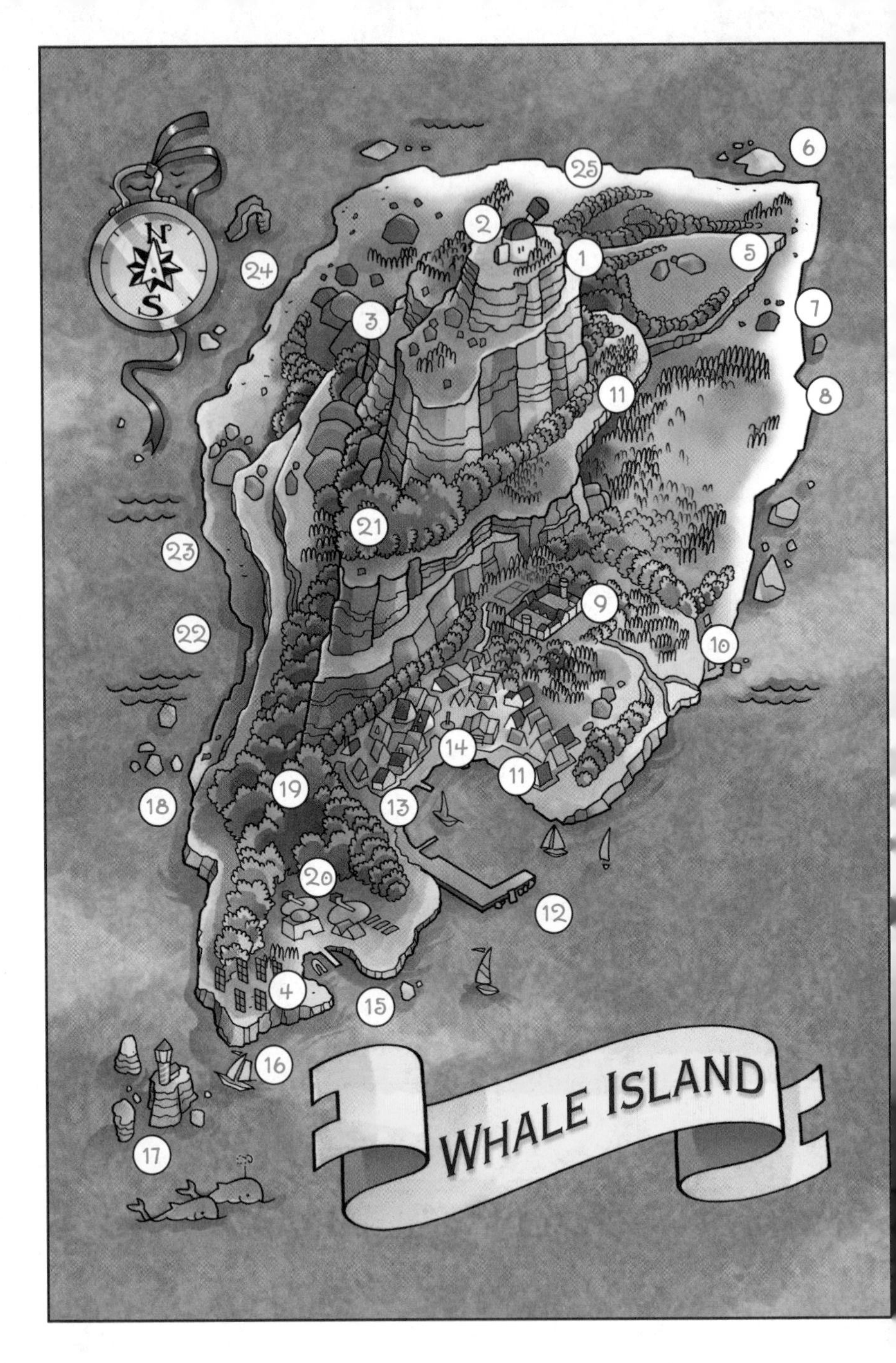
N
S
25
6
2
1
5
24
3
7
11
8
21
23
9
22
10
14
11
19
18
13
20
12
4
15
16
17
WHALE ISLAND

MAP OF WHALE ISLAND

1. Falcon Peak
2. Observatory
3. Mount Landslide
4. Solar Energy Plant
5. Ram Plain
6. Very Windy Point
7. Turtle Beach
8. Beachy Beach
9. Mouseford Academy
10. Kneecap River
11. Mariner's Inn
12. Port
13. Squid House
14. Town Square
15. Butterfly Bay
16. Mussel Point
17. Lighthouse Cliff
18. Pelican Cliff
19. Nightingale Woods
20. Marine Biology Lab
21. Hawk Woods
22. Windy Grotto
23. Seal Grotto
24. Seagulls Bay
25. Seashell Beach

THANKS FOR READING, AND GOOD-BYE UNTIL OUR NEXT ADVENTURE!

Thea Sisters